This edition published by Parragon Books Ltd in 2015

Parragon Books Ltd
Chartist House
15–17 Trim Street
Bath BA1 1HA, UK
www.parragon.com

ISBN 978-1-4748-1660-1

Printed in China

# CHRISTMAS
# STORYBOOK
## COLLECTION

Bath · New York · Cologne · Melbourne · Delhi
Hong Kong · Shenzhen · Singapore · Amsterdam

# Contents

# The Perfect Gift

Christmas was just a few days away. Geppetto, the old wood-carver, was busy making toy soldiers and pretty dolls for the boys and girls in the village. There seemed to be more toys than usual to make this year. Geppetto was afraid that he wouldn't get all the work done in time.

Geppetto's son, Pinocchio, was eager to help his father. He knew that Geppetto worked harder during the Christmas season than at any other time of the year. While Geppetto worked day and night to make all the toys, Pinocchio, with the help of Jiminy Cricket, decorated the house for the holidays. They put up a tree and strung popcorn on its branches and they hung garlands of holly.

This would be Pinocchio's first Christmas as a real boy, so he wanted it to be very special.

"Jiminy," Pinocchio said, "I want to find the perfect gift for Geppetto. He should have something special. Will you help me?"

"Hmm," Jiminy said. "Well, if you ask me—"

"Maybe he would like a new knife to carve with?" Pinocchio said. He thought that he might not have enough money for that. "Oh, what about some warm gloves? He could use them when he goes out on cold nights to deliver toys."

"You know, Pinocchio, I wonder if a better gift would be—" Jiminy began.

"Socks!" Pinocchio cried. "Or a new hat! Come on, Jiminy, let's go to the shops and see what we can find." Pinocchio hurried out of the door. Jiminy had to run to keep up.

In the shops, Pinocchio looked at socks, warm hats, gloves, scarves and even a warm woollen coat. Everything was too small, too expensive, or too ordinary. Pinocchio wanted to find something special.

By Christmas Eve, Pinocchio still hadn't found the perfect gift for Geppetto. He felt sad.

"What am I going to do?" he asked Jiminy.

"Well, I do have this idea," the cricket said.

"Really?" Pinocchio asked. "Please tell me!"

Jiminy sat him at the table and handed him a quill pen.

"You want to give your father something he really needs?"

"I sure do." Pinocchio beamed.

"Write this," Jiminy said. "'Dear Geppetto, my gift to you is an extra pair of hands and an extra-willing heart. Love, Pinocchio.'"

When Pinocchio finished writing, he looked up at Jiminy. "Now what?" he asked.

"Now, you put the note in here." Jiminy held out a box. Pinocchio dropped the note in. Then, Jiminy wrapped the package with bright paper and a big bow.

"Geppetto will be very happy with this gift," Jiminy said.

"But it's just a scrap of paper," Pinocchio said. "What sort of a gift is that?"

Jiminy smiled. "You might be surprised."

Geppetto took a break from his work to share a Christmas Eve dinner with his son. After the meal, Pinocchio gave Geppetto his gift.

"What's this?" he asked.

"Your Christmas present," Pinocchio replied. "I hope you like it."

Geppetto untied the bow and tore the wrapping paper away.

"Why… this is the perfect present!" he exclaimed. "I could use an extra pair of hands in my workshop. How did you know, Pinocchio?"

Pinocchio just smiled. Jiminy had been right – he was surprised at how much joy his gift brought to his father.

"I'm glad to help," Pinocchio said. "I can start right now if you want."

Pinocchio cleared away the dinner dishes from the table, washed them and put them away. Then, he went to Geppetto's workshop. He swept up the wood shavings and boxed and wrapped the new toys. He made labels for each box so that Geppetto would know who each gift was for.

When Geppetto set out to deliver the last of the gifts, Pinocchio went up to bed. He was tired after helping his father all night. He was very pleased that he had made his father so happy. As he drifted off to sleep, he promised himself that he would help out more often.

That night, the Blue Fairy appeared.

"Because you have been so thoughtful this year, I have come to grant you one very special Christmas wish," she said. "Think carefully about what you want."

Pinocchio thought about the many things that he could ask for. But he still only wanted one thing.

"I want to give Geppetto the perfect Christmas gift," he told the Blue Fairy. "Something that he will love forever."

The Blue Fairy smiled. She knew just what the perfect present would be. "You are a very kind and loving boy, Pinocchio," she said. "I'm sure Geppetto will treasure this gift for years to come."

The next morning, Geppetto woke up early. He quietly went downstairs to light the fire and make breakfast. He was so happy that Pinocchio had helped him the night before, that he wanted to surprise his son. He wanted Pinocchio's first Christmas to be special.

Geppetto went to place his gifts for Pinocchio under the tree. He had carved a beautiful toy rocking horse and had crafted a playful jack-in-the-box. When he looked at the tree, he paused. Then, he gasped.

A puppet that looked exactly like his son hung from the branches.

"My dear Pinocchio!" Geppetto said with a smile.

He examined the puppet. It looked just like a puppet he had made a long time ago. One lonely night, he had made a wish on the Wishing Star that the puppet would turn into a real boy. The Blue Fairy had granted his wish and that was when Pinocchio the puppet had become his son.

When Pinocchio heard his father, he and Jiminy ran downstairs. "Merry Christmas," he shouted.

Geppetto sat in his favourite chair, holding the puppet. "My gift! How did you make it?"

Pinocchio stared at the copy of the puppet he used to be. He smiled. The Blue Fairy had chosen the perfect present for his father.

"Puppet Pinocchio was my favourite creation," Geppetto said. "Oh, how I've missed him."

A frown appeared on Pinocchio's face. "You have?" he asked. "Have I disappointed you?"

Geppetto laughed. "Not at all, son. You've been perfect in every way. This toy reminds me of how very much I wanted a real son. He reminds me of how happy I am to have you."

Pinocchio smiled. He went over to the puppet and looked at it closely. He felt as if he was looking into a mirror – the puppet had the same dark hair and blue eyes that he did.

Geppetto stood up and started dancing with the puppet and singing. Pinocchio clapped along. He was thrilled that his father was so happy.

Stopping to catch his breath, Geppetto looked at his son and said, "No one has ever thought to give me a toy of my own to play with because I'm a toy maker. You understand how much I love toys, Pinocchio. Thank you, son."

"See," Jiminy whispered to Pinocchio, "I told you that you would be surprised and now you've been surprised twice!"

Pinocchio nodded as he watched his father dance with the puppet some more. Then, he went over and danced beside the puppet that looked so much like him.

Geppetto held out the strings for Pinocchio so that he could try to make the puppet dance for himself. It was difficult, because the puppet was the same size as Pinocchio, but he didn't care. He was happy to share this moment with his father.

A little later, Pinocchio opened the gifts that Geppetto had placed under the tree for him. He laughed as the jack-in-the-box popped up and he rocked the small wooden horse across the floor. However, the best present that he'd received had come from the Blue Fairy. He would never forget the smile on his father's face. He hoped that they would share many more holidays just like this one.

# Lady and the TRAMP

# Lady's Christmas Surprise

It was the week before Christmas. Tramp and the puppies gathered beneath Jim and Darling's brightly decorated tree.

"You all know what holiday is coming up, right?" Tramp asked, his eyes twinkling.

"Of course, Dad," Scamp said. He was excited. Christmas was the puppies' favourite holiday. Lots of guests stopped by to wish Jim and Darling a happy holiday.

However, the best part of Christmas was the presents. The puppies got to help choose a special gift for each of their parents. They loved being trusted with two such important surprises.

"Do any of you kids know what your mother would like for Christmas?" Tramp asked.

"How about a steak from Tony's Restaurant?" Annette said.

Tramp shook his head. "We can do better than that."

"We need to give her something special," said Colette, "to show her how much we love her."

"Why don't you ask her what she'd like?" said Scamp, his voice muffled. He was chewing on a bow.

"We want to surprise her," Tramp reminded his son. He nudged him away from the presents. "That's the fun of Christmas."

"Maybe we'll find something on our walk today," Annette said.

Tramp thought that was a good idea. While Lady was taking a nap, he took the kids into town to look for the perfect present.

The village bustled with shoppers, their carriage wheels carving deep ruts in the snowy road.

The dogs rambled up and down the avenue, looking in all the shop windows. They saw sweaters, cushions, brush and comb sets, bowls and collars. But Tramp knew that none of these things were the perfect gift for Lady. He wanted to find her something special. Something that she would enjoy and that no other dog would have.

Tramp and the puppies kept looking into the shop windows and they peeked at the packages that all the people were carrying. All they needed was one really good idea.

When the Sun started to sink in the sky, Tramp turned to the puppies and said, "We'd better head for the alleys and dig something from the rubbish."

As they crossed the road, Tramp noticed something sparkling in the snow. It was much brighter than an icicle. He turned it over with his paw.

"Holy hambones!" he cried. It was a gold and diamond necklace!

"What a bunch of rocks!" exclaimed Scamp.

"What a good stroke of luck!" remarked Annette.

"Just the right size for Mother!" added Colette.

Tramp smiled and then scooped up the necklace with his mouth. They'd found the perfect gift. He knew it would look beautiful on Lady.

Suddenly, Tramp dropped the necklace into the snow. It sparkled in the icy crystals. He frowned.

"What's the matter?" Scamp asked.

"This isn't right," Tramp muttered. Then he looked at his children. "Sorry, kids, but we have to return the necklace. It's not ours to take."

"But where would we go to return it?" Colette asked.

"Yeah, it was just here in the snow," Annette said. "How would we even find the owner?"

"I say finders keepers!" Scamp cried.

"Come on now, kids," Tramp said. "We can take it to the police. They'll know who to return it to."

With the puppies following, he bounded down the street to the station.

Inside, officers hurried around taking phone calls and writing reports.

"Stay close, kids," Tramp whispered to the puppies. "I don't want to lose you in the crowd."

Tramp trotted up to the front desk, with the puppies following behind. He dropped the necklace in front of the policeman in charge.

"What's this?" the officer said as he looked at the dog and then back to the necklace on the desk. He picked up the necklace and looked at the sparkling jewels.

Tramp panted and wagged his tail. The puppies stood eagerly beside him. Yip! Yip!

"You found it?" the officer asked.

Tramp nodded.

"Good dog!" he exclaimed.

The policeman took the necklace and began filling out his report while Tramp and the puppies watched.

At that moment, a woman rushed into the station. "Help!" she cried. "My necklace is gone! I'm offering a reward for its return."

The policeman smiled at the woman. Then, he held out the necklace. "Is this yours?" he asked. He pointed to Tramp. "This dog found it on the street and brought it here."

The woman gasped. "Thank you," she said. She scratched Tramp behind his ear. "How can I repay you?"

Woof! Tramp looked at the necklace.

"A new collar," she said. "That's it!"

She took Tramp and the puppies to the shop next door. Tramp walked up to the counter and picked up a gold collar with green stones that looked just like the woman's necklace.

"I'll take that one," the woman told the shopkeeper.

On Christmas morning Lady tore open the gift.

"You shouldn't have!" Her eyes sparkled like the green stones.

When Darling fastened the collar around Lady's neck, she pranced around the room as if she were a show dog.

"I love my new collar," Lady said. "What a wonderful Christmas surprise! But I love my family even more." She nuzzled Tramp and each of the puppies.

"Merry Christmas, Mother," said the puppies.

And it was a very merry Christmas, indeed.

# Bambi

# The Wonderful Winter Tree

**B**ambi awoke one morning to find that the whole world was covered in a soft white blanket.

"What is it, Mother?" Bambi asked as he gazed around in wonder.

"This is snow," replied his mother. "It means winter is upon us."

"Snow!" said Bambi. He took a cautious step… and then another

… and another. He felt the icy crystals crunch underneath his hooves. He looked back at the tiny tracks he had made.

"I like snow!" Bambi said.

"Snow is pretty to look at," his mother told him, "but it makes winter hard for all the animals."

Bambi was about to ask her why winter was harder than other seasons, but just then, his friend Thumper came hopping over.

"Hiya, Bambi!" said the bunny. "Come on! Let's go sliding!" He led Bambi to the pond, which was frozen solid.

Thumper slapped at the ice with his foot. "Come on! It's all right," he told Bambi. "See! The water's stiff!"

Bambi saw his friend, Flower the skunk.

"You want to come sliding?" Bambi called, running over. "Thumper says the water's stiff."

Flower shook his head. "No thanks. I'm off to my den. I'm going to sleep through the winter." He yawned. "Goodbye, Bambi," he said.

"'Bye, Flower," said Bambi. Then he spied another friend, a squirrel, scurrying up an oak tree.

"The pond is stiff, Squirrel," called Bambi. "Want to come sliding with me?"

"Thanks," replied the squirrel as he ducked into a hollow in the tree, "but I have to store nuts for the long winter." He showed Bambi the pile he had already collected. "No sliding for me today."

So, Bambi headed back to Thumper and the ice-covered pond by himself.

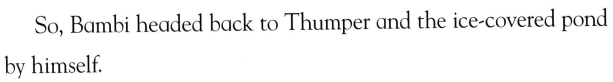

By that time, Thumper was sliding across the ice with some of his sisters. They made it look so easy, but when Bambi stepped on the ice, he lost his balance straight away. His hooves went sliding in four different directions!

"Kind of wobbly, aren't ya," said Thumper. He laughed. "Come on, Bambi. You can do it!"

Bambi wasn't so sure. It seemed that sliding across the stiff water wasn't quite as much fun for deer as it was for rabbits. And it also made him hungry. He said goodbye to the bunnies and went back to find his mother.

"Mother, I'm hungry," Bambi told her.

In the spring, summer and autumn, they had been able to find food almost anywhere they looked. Now that it was winter, Bambi could see that finding food wasn't so easy. There were no leaves on the trees and the grass was covered with snow and ice. The snow was so cold that when he poked through it, Bambi thought his nose might freeze.

At last, Bambi's mother uncovered a small patch of grass and Bambi nibbled it eagerly.

Then, Bambi curled up with his mother for a nap. The ground was hard and cold, and the wind was chilly. Bambi was grateful to have his mother there to keep him warm.

"Is this why the birds fly south and why our other friends sleep through the winter?" Bambi asked her.

His mother nodded and snuggled even closer. "But don't worry, Bambi," she told him. "Winter doesn't last forever."

By the end of December, there seemed nothing left in the forest for Bambi to eat but bitter bark. The days grew short and the nights grew long, and throughout them, Bambi's stomach rumbled. Then one day, something truly amazing happened.

Thumper was the first to see it. "Hey, Bambi!" he shouted. "Would you look at that tree!"

Bambi followed Thumper's paw. He could not believe his eyes.

There before them was a tall pine tree unlike any Bambi had ever seen. It was draped with strings of bright berries and yummy popcorn, and from the end of each branch hung a ripe, juicy apple. Bambi thought that the most wonderful thing was the gold star at the very top.

"Mother!" exclaimed Bambi. "Look what Thumper found!"

Slowly and cautiously, his mother drew closer. "It can't be...." she whispered. "It seems almost too good to be true."

"What is it, Mother?" Bambi asked her.

"The most beautiful tree in the world," she answered. She smiled down at Bambi. "What a special gift to have on your first Christmas."

"Who left it, Mother?" Bambi asked.

"I don't know," she replied.

"Maybe someone who loves animals," Thumper said, hopping up and down. "This is the best gift ever." He sniffed one of the apples hanging low to the ground.

"Can we share this food with every one of our friends, Mother?" Bambi asked.

"Yeah, and with my sisters, too?" Thumper chimed in.

"I don't see why not," Bambi's mother said. "Christmas is a time to share what we have with those we love."

Bambi and Thumper danced happily around the tree.

"Look at all the popcorn and berries!" Thumper cried. "And look at that star at the tippy-top, too!"

Bambi stopped prancing. He looked up at the golden star at the top of the tree. Then he looked up at the sky above him. The Sun was just beginning to go down. He knew that very soon, there would be a star twinkling in the sky just like the one at the top of the tree. A gentle hush fell over the clearing.

He danced back over to his mother and took a big bite out of one of the juicy green apples. Mmm! he thought. Nothing had ever tasted so good!

Gazing up at the star and at the wonderful winter tree, Bambi could feel a happy, warm glow swelling inside him. There was enough food on the tree to feed all the animals who were hungry. What a magical gift, thought Bambi. Winter was long and hard… and yet wonderful, after all.

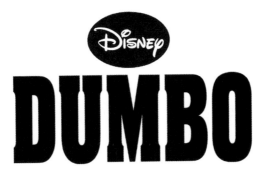

# DUMBO

# The Best Christmas

One December morning, Dumbo the flying elephant woke up to find the circus grounds strangely quiet. He stuck his head outside his tent. Where was everyone?

Then Timothy Mouse appeared. "It's the Christmas holiday," he announced. "Time to sleep late, play in the snow and get ready for the holidays!"

Dumbo looked puzzled.

CLOSED

"Aw, don't tell me you've never heard of Christmas before," Timothy said in disbelief.

"Hey, fellas," he called up to the crows, "come on down here. I need help explaining Christmas to Dumbo."

The birds gathered around the elephant and began to chatter all at once.

"Why, Christmas is packages wrapped up in shiny paper."

"Now wait a minute! What about fancy holiday food?"

"Don't forget a big tree covered in ornaments and lights."

"And music! You can't have Christmas without carols!"

"Now do you understand?" Timothy asked Dumbo.

The elephant shook his head. He was even more confused.

"Hmmm," Timothy said, "this is gonna be harder than I thought." He and the crows huddled together and quickly came up with a new plan.

"Dumbo," said Timothy, "forget telling you about Christmas, we're gonna show you!"

Timothy Mouse scampered up onto Dumbo's cap. "Get ready for take-off!" he cried.

The crows took to the sky. Dumbo flapped his ears and followed right behind them. They flew and flew until, finally, a magnificent skyline came into view.

"Welcome to New York City!" Timothy announced. "I can't think of a more Christmassy place – except maybe the North Pole!" Timothy had grown up in New York and he thought it was the best place on Earth.

The little mouse gave Dumbo a tour of the bustling city. He showed the elephant the most festive place in New York first.

"That's Rockefeller Center," Timothy pointed out as they flew over a large tree.

Below, ice skaters glided and twirled around a sparkling outdoor rink. Dumbo couldn't take his eyes off the enormous tree, covered from top to bottom in twinkling lights and pretty decorations.

Timothy could tell that Dumbo was impressed. "What did I tell you?" the mouse asked. "People here don't just deck the halls – they decorate everything!"

Dumbo looked at all the people on the streets, full of holiday cheer. Some carried brightly wrapped packages. Some were singing carols. Everyone was in awe of the great big tree.

The sights and sounds of Christmas made Dumbo feel very happy. He couldn't wait to find out more about the holiday!

Timothy Mouse and Dumbo flew down Fifth Avenue, where the shop windows were filled with beautiful Christmas displays. Dumbo watched the shoppers hurrying around with large bags of presents.

Timothy saw something else.

"Hmm, that's strange," he said. "People keep leaving presents in a box in front of that store over there. Come on, let's go and find out what's going on."

When Dumbo swooped down closer to the crowd, everyone cheered. They had never seen a flying elephant before. Dumbo felt like he was performing in one of his shows.

"What are the presents for?" Timothy Mouse asked a woman. "Is it the store's birthday or something?"

The woman chuckled. Then she explained that the packages were toys for children.

"There's just one problem," she continued. "The snow has slowed down traffic and I don't know how we're going to make all our deliveries on time. The boys and girls will be so disappointed if they don't get their presents this year!"

71

Timothy looked at Dumbo. Dumbo looked at Timothy. "Are you thinking what I'm thinking?" the mouse asked.

Dumbo nodded enthusiastically.

"Lady," said Timothy, "Dumbo and I would be happy to help spread a little Christmas cheer. I know this city like the back of my hand and Dumbo here never needs to worry about stuff like traffic. You can consider those presents as good as delivered!"

The people on the sidewalk cheered. "Thank you, Dumbo," one man said. "I knew Santa had flying reindeer, but I didn't know he had a flying elephant!"

"Shhh," Timothy replied with a mischievous wink. "It's supposed to be a secret!"

Soon Dumbo was given a sack of presents and a long list of names and addresses.

"Ho, ho, ho!" Timothy called out as he and Dumbo flew off.

The pair arrived at their first stop. Through the window, they could see children hanging stockings over the fireplace. When they saw Dumbo and Timothy Mouse they shouted with joy. Timothy handed each child a brightly wrapped present.

"Thank you!" they cried as Dumbo and Timothy flew away. "And Merry Christmas!"

Dumbo and Timothy flew from one house to another. They dropped off dolls and dump trucks, books and building blocks, puppets and puzzles. Every once in a while, the crows took a break from sightseeing to pitch in and sing some Christmas music. They were the funniest carol singers that the kids had ever seen!

Timothy's favourite part was watching the children and their parents when they spied Dumbo outside their windows. They'd blink and rub their eyes, wondering if what they were seeing could possibly be real.

"What's the matter?" Timothy would say playfully. "Haven't you ever seen a flying elephant before?" Then he'd laugh.

Dumbo loved the way that the children's faces lit up when he gave them their presents. It made him feel happy right down to his toes.

"We'll come back to visit them again soon, Dumbo," said Timothy as they headed home. "I promise."

Back at the circus grounds, Timothy and Dumbo settled down for the night.

"So, Dumbo," Timothy asked, "now do you know what Christmas is all about?"

Dumbo wasn't listening, though. He was thinking of all the children he had met that day and how he and Timothy had made them all smile. It had been the best Christmas.

Seeing Dumbo's happy expression, Timothy said, "Yup, I think you do."

The two tired friends soon fell fast asleep. That night, for the first time ever, Dumbo's dreams – and his heart – were filled with the magic of Christmas.

# Lightning's Snow Day

Early one afternoon, Lightning and Mater rolled up to Flo's V8 Café. It was a cold winter day and clouds were gathering in the sky.

"Have you heard?" Flo asked them. "Sheriff says it might snow overnight."

"Snow!" cried Mater. "I love snow!"

Lightning was excited, too. "I've never actually seen snow before," he told Mater.

Mater stopped in his tracks. "Wait. Never? Never ever? Well, dadgum! Now it had *better* snow. We're going to have some winter fun!"

Just then, Sally rode up. She'd heard the weather forecast, too. "If it's cold enough tomorrow, the pond will freeze," she said. "We could go ice-skating!"

Lightning couldn't wait!

Mater and Lightning woke up the next morning to find Radiator Springs covered in snow. *"Woo-eee!"* Mater cried. "It's my best-buddy Lightning McQueen's first-ever snow day!"

The friends went to Luigi's for some new snow tyres. Then they stopped at Flo's for a quick can of warm oil.

"Are you ready to play in the snow?" Mater asked.

"You bet," Lightning answered. "Let's go!"

Lightning and Mater turned into Main Street.

Suddenly, they spotted their friend Ramone. He had painted himself bright blue, with white snowflakes.

"Would you like a new paint job, too?" Ramone asked Lightning.

"That would be great!" Lightning exclaimed. Soon, the race car was sporting a wintery look.

"How do you like your new 'snow style'?" asked Ramone.

"I love it!" said Lightning. "Thanks!"

Mater and Lightning drove to the top of a large hill. "The only way to start a snow day," Mater explained, "is to go snow drifting." With a wink, Mater began rolling. "Race you to the bottom!"

The two cars slipped and slid all the way down the slope. Lightning laughed. He was having a great time.

Later, Lightning and Mater drove over to the pond.
Sarge was there, checking the ice. "Better safe than sorry!"
he called. "Need to make sure it won't crack."

"Crack?" Lightning said nervously. "W-wait a minute.
Can that happen?" He wasn't sure he wanted to go ice-skating
after all.

"Nervous?" Lightning heard a voice say behind him. He turned and saw Sally. "A big-time racer like you must be able to handle a little ice-skating," she said with a smile.

"Uh. . . of course!"
Lightning replied. He followed
Sally out onto the ice. But it was
hard to keep his wheels straight.
Sally giggled. "You know a lot about racing," she teased,
"but you have a few things to learn about skating."

Meanwhile, Mater started a game. "Toot-toot! All aboard the
Mater Express!" he yelled. He pulled Luigi and Guido across the ice
using his hook and cable.

"Are you coming, Lightning?" Sally called.

"You bet!" Lightning replied. "Just let me get my wheels under me."

Just then, the snow began to fall again. "Oh, boy!" Mater exclaimed. "No snow day is complete without catching a snowflake on your tongue."

Lightning stuck out his tongue just like Mater. The cars all tried to catch as many frosty flakes as they could.

"This has been the best day ever," Lightning said to Mater and Sally as they cruised back home.

Little did Lightning know, his snow day wasn't finished yet. Luigi and Guido were waiting behind a tree with a huge pile of snowballs!

*Thwack!* A snowball flew through the air.

"Snowball fight!" Mater cried. "Take cover!"

"Ha-ha!" Lightning laughed as he dodged the snowballs. "They'll never hit me!"

But Mater wasn't so lucky. "Oof. That's going to leave a dent," he said as a snowball hit his roof.

That night, all the cars rolled back into town.

"Did you have a good snow day?" Mater asked.

"It was awesome," Lightning said. "But now that I'm a snow pro, I'll have even more fun tomorrow when I zip past you on that hill."

"Better have a light breakfast," joked Mater, "'cause you'll be eating snow while trying to catch me up."

"You're on!" Lightning grinned.

Everyone gathered at Flo's for some cans of warm oil under the starry winter sky.

"Mmm," said Mater. "There's nothing better than a warm sip to end the perfect snow day. Right, buddy?"

Lightning nodded. "Except maybe sharing it with good friends," he answered.

# Disney·PIXAR
# MONSTERS, INC.

# Christmas Laughs

Mike Wazowski, the green one-eyed monster, was on the Monsters, Inc. Laugh Floor. He couldn't keep from looking at the Laugh Meter. It showed all of the laughs that the monsters had collected by telling kids jokes. The laughs were turned into energy for the city of Monstropolis.

Monsters, Inc. had always been able to collect enough laughs to make sure that the monsters never had to worry about losing power. However, with Christmas around the corner, it seemed as if more and more kids were on holiday. That made it harder to collect laughs.

Mike was worried that there wouldn't be enough power to light up the Christmas tree in the city centre. Everybody looked forward to this Monstropolis tradition!

"Come on, monsters," he called out. "Think funny!"

Mike watched one monster go through a child's wardrobe door. When he came back onto the Laugh Floor, Mike looked at the canister that collected laughs. It wasn't even half full.

Just then, Sulley showed up. The big, furry blue monster
was the president of Monsters, Inc. He was also Mike's best friend.
"How's it going, Mike?" asked Sulley.
"Fine, fine," Mike answered nervously. He didn't want his boss
to know that they were running short on laughs. "That
Christmas tree will be lit up in no time."

Mike saw Sulley peek over at the Laugh
Meter. "I bet there are a lot of kids who
are—" Sulley started.

"No time to talk, buddy," Mike
cut him off. He guided Sulley
towards the door. "Got to get back
to work and collect those laughs."
"Okay," said Sulley. "See
you later."

As soon as Sulley left, Mike called out again, "Let's go, let's go! Collect those laughs! Christmas is just around the corner!"

The monsters worked even harder at being funny and entertaining. One monster even juggled seven plates and spun another plate on his head. The kid watching him broke into giggles and clapped wildly. The laugh canister quickly filled up.

George, a big, furry orange monster went through another child's door. He sat on a stool next to the little girl's bed, holding a microphone in one hand.

"Hey, is this thing on? Hello?" George said, tapping the microphone. "Ready to have some laughs? Good. Why did the monster eat a lightbulb?"

"Why?" the child asked.

"He needed a light snack!" George exclaimed, and the little girl roared with laughter. "Wait, wait! I have more." He told another joke that sent the child into giggles. On the Laugh Floor, Mike watched the canister outside the door fill up.

"Nice work," Mike said when George had finished.

"Thanks," George said. He and Mike looked up at the Laugh Meter on the wall. It was growing steadily, much to everyone's delight.

"We actually might make our goal," Mike said with a hopeful smile.

All of a sudden, Mike and the other monsters watched in horror as the Laugh Meter began to go down instead of up!

"What's going on? What's happening?" Mike said, his voice growing louder.

The laugh wranglers, Smitty and Needleman, weren't sure.

"This has never happened before," said Smitty, the head wrangler.

"Well, don't just stand there," Mike cried. "Fix it!"

The wranglers sprang into action. After a while, they discovered a leak in the laugh tank, where all the laughs were stored.

The monsters on the Laugh Floor were worried. They wondered if all of their hard work had been for nothing.

"Ho, ho, ho!" came a cheerful voice.

Mike looked up and saw Santa Claus walking onto the floor. Then he realized that it was Sulley dressed in a Santa suit.

"I'm just getting into the Christmas spirit," Sulley explained. Then he looked around. "It looks like I'm the only one. What's going on?"

Mike explained the problem. "But I've got everything under control, Santa, er, Sulley."

"I'm sure you do," Sulley replied. "I'm just going to see if there's anything I can do to help."

Sulley followed Mike into the basement of Monsters, Inc., where the laugh wranglers were hard at work. Everyone wanted to get the laugh tank fixed as soon as possible and time was running out. The tree-lighting ceremony was only a few hours away!

The wranglers couldn't agree on how to fix the problem.

"Anything I can do?" Sulley asked.

"One of the pipes that leads into the laugh tank has burst," explained Smitty. "We need to tie it off, but none of our tools are strong enough to turn the pipe."

Hmm… said Sulley, scratching his head.

Then, Mike had a great idea. "Why not actually tie it off?" Since Sulley was so strong, he could bend that pipe right into a pretzel shape!

Sulley was willing to give it a try. Mike stood by his side and coached him.

It worked! The pipe stopped leaking!

Mike and Sulley headed back up to the Laugh Floor. All the monsters congratulated Sulley!

Mike wondered why no one was thanking him. It had been his idea, after all! But there was no time to think about that now.

"We're back up and running!" Mike announced. "Let's make some laughs!"

All the monsters got to work. They knew they'd have to work extra hard to make up for all the lost laughs.

Sulley decided to jump in and help. "Hey, we've only got a couple of hours to get the tree lit," he said to Mike.

Still dressed as Santa, Sulley went through a child's wardrobe door.

When he came back onto the Laugh Floor, he looked up at the Laugh Meter on the wall. It was increasing, but slowly.

"We've got to make it," Sulley whispered to Mike.

Finally, the Laugh Meter was back up to the level it had been before the leak. Sulley looked at the clock on the wall and frowned. It was only thirty minutes until the tree-lighting ceremony.

Suddenly, Sulley had an idea. "The only way we're going to make our laugh quota is to get some really over-the-top laughs."

Mike nodded in agreement.

"We need a grand slam here," continued Sulley. "We need a special kind of monster. One with perfect timing… star quality… a natural at comedy… a one-eyed sensation."

Mike realized what Sulley was trying to do. He crossed his arms and shook his head. "No, Sulley. Absolutely not."

"The Christmas tree lighting is only half an hour away," Sulley told him. "Come on, Mike. The whole city is depending on you."

That was all Mike needed to hear. "You're right. Let's do it!" he said. "But you're coming with me!"

Sulley and Mike went through a door together. Sulley was still dressed as Santa and Mike had dressed up as an elf. To their delight, a little girls' sleepover was going on!

Mike started with some of his best jokes. "Hey, Sulley, I've got to walk twenty-five miles to get home."

"Why don't you take a train?" Sulley asked, playing along.

"I did once, but my mother made me give it back!" Mike said.

The kids in the room laughed, but not as hard as the monsters had hoped. After a few more jokes, Mike realized he'd have to try something else. He picked up the sack of toys that Sulley had brought in, but it was far too heavy for him.

"Whoa!!" he exclaimed as he tripped. He landed upside down and the sack of toys spilled out around him. He sat up with a doll draped over his head and a toy race car stuck to his foot.

The kids roared with laughter. They begged for more and Mike happily tumbled and tripped for them again.

Mike and Sulley made it back onto the Laugh Floor in time to watch the Laugh Meter hit its limit!

At the tree-lighting ceremony, Mike and Sulley stood proudly in the front of the crowd.

Sulley leant over and whispered in Mike's ear, "You did a great job. Thank you."

Mike smiled. "You know what I always say: funny doesn't grow on trees. When you got it, you got it. And I got it."

Sulley laughed. He was happy Mike had it – and shared it. It was going to be a bright Christmas, after all.

# Winnie the Pooh

# The Sweetest Christmas

One snowy Christmas Eve, Winnie the Pooh looked up and down, in and out, and all around his house.

He had a tree set up in his living room. It was decorated with some candles in honey pots.

Pooh looked at the tree and tapped his head.

"Something seems to be missing," he said.

He walked over to the window and peered outside. Then, he walked back to the tree and thought some more.

Suddenly, a knocking sound startled Pooh. *Rap-a-tap-tap!* He turned towards his front door.

"Maybe whatever it is I can't remember I'm missing is outside my door," Pooh said.

When Pooh opened the door, he found a small snowman on his front step.

"H-h-he-l-l-l-o, P-Pooh B-Bear," the snowman said as he shivered.

Pooh thought the voice sounded very familiar. He invited the snowman inside.

After standing beside the fire for a few minutes, the snowman began to melt. The more he melted, the more he started to look like Piglet!

"Oh, my," said Pooh. He was happy to see his friend where there used to be a snowman.

"Oh, my," said Piglet. Now that the snow had melted off him, he could see Pooh's glowing Christmas tree.

"Are you going to string popcorn for your tree?" Piglet asked.

"There was popcorn and string," Pooh admitted. "But now there is only string."

Pooh thought some more, wondering if popcorn was what he'd forgotten. But that wasn't it, either.

"Then we can use the string to wrap the presents you're giving," Piglet said.

Something began to tickle at Pooh's brain. It was the something missing that he hadn't been able to remember.

"I forgot to get presents!" Pooh exclaimed.

"Don't worry, Pooh," Piglet said. "I'm sure you'll think of something."

Soon it was time for Piglet to go home and wrap his own presents. He said goodbye to his friend and went back out into the cold, snowy night.

Pooh stood beside his tree and tapped his head while he thought. Where could he find presents for his friends? It was already Christmas Eve. Was it too late?

He thought some more. He sat down in his cosy chair. Then he got up and had a small smackerel of honey. He peered out the window and watched the snow fall.

Then he had an idea.

He still didn't know what to do about the presents he'd forgotten, but he knew where to find help.

"Hello!" Pooh called as he knocked on Christopher Robin's door.

Christopher Robin opened the door and smiled when he saw the visitor.

"Come in, Pooh Bear," he said. "Merry Christmas! Why do you look so sad on the most wonderful night of the year?"

Pooh was just about to explain about the forgotten presents when something caught his eye. He pointed at the stockings over the fireplace. "What are those for?" he asked.

"Those are stockings to hold Christmas presents," explained Christopher Robin.

"But Christopher Robin," Pooh said, "what if someone forgot to find presents for his friends? And what if that same someone doesn't have stockings to hang because he doesn't wear any?"

Pooh looked down at his bare feet, then back up at Christopher Robin.

"Silly old bear," Christopher Robin said. He took Pooh up to his room. They dug through his drawers until Pooh found seven stockings.

"Thank you, Christopher Robin," Pooh said. He smiled. He'd picked a stocking for each of his friends to put their presents in: purple for Piglet, red-and-white striped for Tigger, orange for Rabbit, yellow for Eeyore, maroon for Gopher and blue for Owl. He also had one for him to hang over his fireplace.

He hurried off to deliver the stockings to his friends. As he walked through the Hundred-Acre Wood, he thought about the presents he still needed for the stockings.

"I will get the presents later," Pooh said to himself. "The stockings come first."

Pooh stopped at each of his friends' houses. Everyone was asleep. He quietly hung the stockings where his friends would find them. Each one had a tag that read: FROM POOH.

When Pooh got back to his house, he climbed into his cosy chair in front of a roaring fire.

"Now I must think about presents for my friends," he said.

Pooh was tired from finding the stockings and delivering them to his friends' houses. Before he knew it, his thinking turned into dreaming. He was fast asleep.

The next morning, Pooh awoke to a loud thumping noise.
*Thump-a-bump-bump!*

"I wonder who that could be," he said. He climbed out of
his chair and opened the door.

"Merry Christmas, Pooh!" his friends cried.

There on Pooh's doorstep stood Tigger, Rabbit, Piglet, Owl, Eeyore and Gopher. They were each carrying the stocking from Pooh.

Pooh scratched his head. All of a sudden he remembered what had happened the night before. He had fallen asleep before giving presents to his friends!

"Oh, bother," he said. Then he realized that his friends were all talking at once. They were thanking him for their gifts!

"No more cold ears in the winter with my new cap," Piglet said.

"My stripedy sleeping bag is tigger-ific!" exclaimed Tigger.

"So is my new carrot cover," Rabbit said.

"This rock-collecting bag will sure make work go faster," Gopher said.

Eeyore swished his tail to show Pooh his new tail-warmer. "No one's ever given me such a useful gift before," he said.

Owl told Pooh his new wind sock would help him with the day's weather report.

Pooh looked at his friends. They were very happy with their stockings, even though there weren't any presents in them!

"Something very nice is going on," Pooh said.

"It is very nice, Pooh Bear," Piglet said.

"It's called Christmas, buddy bear," Tigger said. He patted Pooh on the back.

"Chris-mess?" Lucky asked. "It does look like a mess." He wagged his tail.

The parlour floor was covered with pine needles, boxes of ornaments, tinsel garlands and strings of small lights.

Anita was waiting in the parlour to help Roger and Nanny. The puppies looked on in awe as their human pets began acting very strangely. Roger hung shiny coloured globes on the branches. Anita was winding a garland around the tree.

When the tree was finished and the room tidied, Roger flipped a switch. The lights and shiny ornaments cast a magical glow about the room. The puppies stared wide-eyed at the tree.

That night, when Pongo and Perdita tucked the puppies into their basket, they told them all about Christmas.

"It's a time when people show their families and friends how much they care for them," Pongo said. He explained how humans sent cards, baked cookies and fruitcakes and sang festive carols.

"It may sound strange, but you'll grow to love the holiday season," Perdita said. She nuzzled Patch, who let out a yawn.

"Especially the beef bones left over from dinner," Pongo added.

"Bones?" Patch said, perking up. His father smiled.

"And that's not all," Perdita continued. "On Christmas Eve, after everyone's in bed, people sneak presents under the tree."

"Presents?" all the puppies said at once.

"What kind of presents?" Patch asked. "Can you wish for them?"

"I'd wish for a new bed," Lucky said as he climbed into the basket that he shared with his brothers and sisters.

"Why do people put presents under the tree?" Pepper asked.

"Christmas is about giving," Pongo told the puppies. "People give presents to their friends and family to show how much they love them."

"I wonder if we will get any presents?" said Rolly.

"Maybe," Perdita replied. "Anita gave me a new collar last year."

"And I got a red ball," said Pongo.

"I hope someone loves us," said Penny.

"You are all loved, whether or not there are presents under the tree," Perdita said. "Now time for bed. Tomorrow is a big day."

On Christmas morning, the puppies woke at dawn. They crept into the parlour. Sure enough, there were piles of brightly wrapped packages under the tree.

"We are loved!" Freckles cried.

The puppies dived into the pile of presents. They tossed the packages around and ripped and tore at the coloured paper.

"Christmas is fun!" Rolly exclaimed as he shook some wrapping paper out of his mouth.

Lucky pulled open a box. "Perfume?" he said and wrinkled his nose.

Penny dragged a spotted necktie out of some tissue paper. "What do I need with more spots?"

Freckles held up a lace handkerchief. "What is this for?" he asked.

Just then, they heard Roger and Anita's voices in the hallway.

The puppies looked at each other in alarm.

"Let's get out of here!" Rolly said. The puppies scampered around the room, hiding behind the sofa, under the chairs and in the folds of the curtains.

The puppies trembled when they heard Roger's footsteps.

He stopped in the doorway. "What on Earth?" he said.

Anita walked up beside him. "Oh, dear!" she cried.

"Perdita, Pongo," Roger called out.

"Where are you?"

The puppies
heard the click of
their parents' claws
on the wooden floor as
they scurried towards
the parlour.

When they came
into the room, Pongo
said, "Woof!"

And Perdita
repeated, "Woof!"

The puppies looked at each other uncertainly. "We're in for it now," Lucky whispered.

Then they heard something very strange. Anita started to laugh.

Roger said, with a chuckle, "Looks like we had some help opening our gifts."

"Wasn't that kind of the puppies!" Nanny said, as she walked into the room and saw the mess of paper and ribbon.

"I wonder where they've gone off to," Roger said with a twinkle in his eye. "Here, pups!"

"There are still so many boxes to unwrap," Anita said, shaking her head. "I do wish they'd come and help."

The puppies looked around at each other in their hiding places. Then, one by one, they crept out from under the chairs and behind the sofa.

They gathered around the tree as Roger pulled more packages from under the branches. "Go for it, boys and girls!"

Yip! Yip! The puppies tore into the bright wrappings and the tangled ribbons. They crunched cardboard and rolled around in the crinkly papers. Patch hopped into an empty box to hide. When Lucky started to tear at the top of the box, Patch popped up with a playful, "Woof!"

Pongo and Perdita looked at each other. "Shall we join them?" whispered Pongo.

"This is their first Christmas," Perdita replied. "Let them have their fun."

When the puppies grew tired of rolling around in the wrapping paper, Anita brought out a large basket.

"Sorry we didn't have time to wrap these," she said. "But then…" She smiled. "… maybe you've done enough work for today."

She handed each puppy a squeaky toy.

From the bottom of the basket she pulled out two Christmas jumpers for Pongo and Perdita.

"Anita knitted them herself," said Roger with pride.

That evening, after Christmas dinner was over, the puppies were still full of energy. They weren't ready to go to bed.

"We like Christmas!" said Pepper.

"We like our toys!" said Rolly.

"We like tissue paper!" said Patch.

"But remember what we told you about Christmas?" Perdita asked. She nudged her children towards their basket. "It's a time for giving."

"It's also about forgiving," Pongo said gently. "You were lucky that Roger and Anita weren't upset that you unwrapped their presents."

The puppies' heads drooped a little.

"We're lucky we have two wonderful humans," Perdita said softly. "That is the best present we could ask for."

The puppies raised their eyes to their mother hopefully.

"We are loved," Penny said. She smiled.

"You are all, each and every one of you, loved," Perdita assured her children.

"And that's what Christmas is really all about," Pongo said as the puppies drifted off to sleep.

# THE END